P9-ARJ-545

UNiCORN ACADEMY
TREASURE HUNT

Lyra rode Misty into the cave. Misty stepped carefully over the rubble, her hooves slipping and sliding. "Follow us, everyone," Lyra said in excitement, "and keep your eyes open for the next piece of the map!"

LOOK OUT FOR MORE ADVENTURES WITH

UNICORN ACADEMY

TREASURE HUNT

Lyra and Misty

Evie and Sunshine

Ivy and Flame

Sienna and Sparkle

UNICORN ACADEMY

TREASURE HUNT 1

Lyra
and
Misty

JULIE SYKES

illustrated by LUCY TRUMAN

A STEPPING STONE BOOK™

Random House · New York

This is a work of fiction. Names, characters, places, and incidents either are
the product of the author's imagination or are used fictitiously.
Any resemblance to actual persons, living or dead, events,
or locales is entirely coincidental.

Text copyright © 2021 by Julie Sykes and Linda Chapman
Cover art and interior illustrations copyright © 2021 by Lucy Truman

All rights reserved. Published in the United States by Random House
Children's Books, a division of Penguin Random House LLC, New York.
Originally published in paperback in the United Kingdom by
Nosy Crow Ltd, London, in 2021.

Random House and the colophon are registered trademarks and
A Stepping Stone Book and the colophon are trademarks of
Penguin Random House LLC.

Visit us on the Web! rhcbooks.com

Educators and librarians, for a variety of teaching tools, visit us at
RHTeachersLibrarians.com

Library of Congress Cataloging-in-Publication Data
Names: Sykes, Julie, author. | Truman, Lucy, illustrator.
Title: Lyra and Misty / Julie Sykes; illustrated by Lucy Truman.
Description: First American edition. | New York: Random House, 2023. |
Series: Unicorn Academy: Treasure hunt; 1 | "A Stepping Stone book." |
Audience: Ages 6–9. | Summary: Lyra is excited to start school at Unicorn
Academy with her unicorn, Misty, but when she and her friends find a piece of
a treasure map, they must solve the clues to find the next piece—
and the hidden treasure—before someone else does.
Identifiers: LCCN 2022039008 (print) | LCCN 2022039009 (ebook) |
ISBN 978-0-593-57142-2 (trade paperback) | ISBN 978-0-593-57144-6 (ebook) |
Subjects: CYAC: Unicorns—Fiction. | Magic—Fiction. |
Buried treasure—Fiction. | Boarding schools—Fiction. | Schools—Fiction.
Classification: LCC PZ7.S98325 Ly 2023 (print) | LCC PZ7.S98325 (ebook) |
DDC [Fic]—dc23

Printed in the United States of America
10 9 8 7 6 5 4 3 2 1
First American Edition

Random House Children's Books supports the First Amendment
and celebrates the right to read.

To Elsie. May all your dreams sparkle
and take you to the stars!

CHAPTER 1

It was a frosty afternoon, and the new students at Unicorn Academy were chatting and laughing as they groomed their unicorns. Lyra pushed her long light-brown hair behind her ears and put down her brush. "Now for your hooves," she said to her unicorn, Misty. "Would you like gold, purple, or pink hoof polish?"

Misty had been staring into the distance, lost in thought. She blinked. "Oh . . . um . . . I don't mind," she said, nuzzling Lyra. "You choose. I'm not very good at making decisions."

"Well, I love making decisions, so we're a

perfect match!" Lyra said, putting her arms around Misty and breathing in her sweet unicorn smell. "Let's use gold!"

Misty was a very pretty snow-white unicorn patterned with flowers of purple and spring green. Lyra had been so happy when Ms. Nettles, the

academy's head teacher, had put them together in the pairing ceremony yesterday.

Lyra picked up the tub of sparkly gold hoof polish and a brush. "I still can't believe I'm actually here at Unicorn Academy," she said happily.

She glanced around her. The academy stables were clean and shiny, with stalls for the unicorns on either side of the wide aisles. Automated trolleys ran up and down the aisles carrying bales of straw and buckets of sky berries, the unicorns' favorite food. The drinking water came from silver troughs that magically filled with multi-colored water from Sparkle Lake.

Lyra had wanted to go to the academy for as long as she could remember. Her cousin Scarlett had been a student a few years ago, and she had told Lyra all about the amazing adventures she'd had with her friends and their unicorns.

I am definitely *going to have adventures while I'm here*, Lyra thought as she painted Misty's hooves.

Misty gave Lyra a look from under her long eyelashes. "Are . . . are you missing your family at all, Lyra?"

Lyra paused. She had thought she would miss her parents and sister, but there had been so much going on from the moment she'd arrived at the academy that she hadn't missed home much at all. "No, not really," she admitted.

Misty hung her head, and Lyra wondered if Misty was homesick. She decided to distract her by talking about something different. "I wonder what magical power you'll have," she said, "and when you'll discover it. It'll be so cool to be able to do magic!"

Before they could graduate and become guardians of Unicorn Island, students had to bond with their unicorn and each unicorn had to discover

their magical power. Sometimes students and their unicorns needed more time to complete everything and returned for a second year.

"I really hope you have the power to do something super exciting, like being able to fly or turn invisible," Lyra continued. "Those powers would be awesome!" She glanced across the aisle to where Sienna, who was also in Ruby dorm, was braiding her unicorn's mane with blue and purple ribbons. "Hey, Sienna, if Sparkle could have any magical power, what would you choose?"

Sienna was tall with corkscrew curls that reached her shoulders. Her brown eyes lit up as she considered the question. "I'd choose for Sparkle to be able to gallop at the speed of light so we could beat everyone whenever we raced!"

Sparkle, a very athletic unicorn, stamped his hoof and said, "That would be fun!"

Sienna's words gave Lyra an idea. "Why don't we go have some races? Or, even better, go exploring. Ivy? Evie?" she shouted to the other two girls in their dorm. "What do you think? Shall we go for a Ruby dorm ride?"

Evie was carrying a bucket of water toward her unicorn, Sunshine. She looked around as Lyra called her name and tripped over her feet. She cried out as she fell, dropping the bucket and sending water splashing everywhere.

"Evie! Are you okay?" cried Ivy.

"I'm fine," said Evie, blushing bright red as the girls all ran over to help her up. "I'm so clumsy," she groaned. "Look at this mess." She tried to grab a nearby broom to sweep the water away, but her fingers fumbled with the handle and the broom fell into Sienna. She gasped. "Oh no! Sorry!"

"No problem," said Sienna with a grin. "But maybe I'll do the sweeping!"

"Yes, you should go get some dry clothes," said Ivy to Evie. "You're soaked."

"And when you come back, we can all go exploring!" Lyra said eagerly. "There are so many places we haven't been yet: the maze, the cross-country course, the woods—"

"What about the Safari Trail? I want to see that," interrupted Ivy. "There are supposed to be some really interesting animals there."

"I've heard the woods are filled with some incredible creatures," said Lyra. She'd also heard the woods were dangerous, and the thought of

checking them out made excitement fizz through her.

"Aren't they off-limits?" asked Sienna.

"We won't go inside. We'll just go to the edge and take a look," said Lyra with a grin. "I think it's time for Ruby dorm to go on an adventure!"

CHAPTER 2

A little while later, the four girls trotted their unicorns away from the stables. The air was frosty, and the grass crunched under the unicorns' hooves as they rode around the edge of Sparkle Lake.

Sparkle Lake's water had magical properties. It sprang up from the center of the earth, ran through a fountain in the middle of the lake, and then flowed around the island. The water helped all the people, plants, and animals on the island flourish, and it also strengthened the unicorns' magic.

Lyra grinned as they left the lake and headed toward the lush green meadows. Here she was, with her own unicorn, out on an adventure at last! She loved exploring. When she was older, she wanted to be an archaeologist who discovered unknown places and found rare artifacts. She couldn't think of a more fun job!

"So where are we going?" Sienna asked.

"The woods," said Lyra.

"Are you sure, Lyra?" said Misty. "They sound dangerous, and we shouldn't go in if they're off-limits."

"We'll stay on the edge. It'll be fun," said Lyra. "That's if we can find them, of course!"

"You mean we might get lost?" asked Misty.

Lyra ruffled her mane. "Yep! That's the best thing about exploring—you never know what's going to happen!"

"Oh," said Misty, gulping.

"Come on, I'm tired of trotting. Let's canter," said Sienna. "Or, even better, gallop!"

Sienna urged Sparkle on, and they all raced across the grounds and into the meadow. A sparkling, multicolored stream wound through the long grass, and the unicorns stopped to have a refreshing drink.

"Let's have a contest to see who can jump over the widest part of the stream," said Sienna.

"Yes!" agreed Sparkle, playfully splashing Flame, who was drinking next to him. "You're pretty fast, Flame, but I bet I can jump farther than you."

"But I was really looking forward to going to the woods," said Lyra, disappointed.

"I think we should do what the others want, Lyra," said Misty quickly. "Jumping the stream sounds fun!"

Lyra sighed. "Okay."

"Great! I'll start," called Sienna. She and Sparkle galloped toward the stream and soared over it. "Beat that, Lyra!" she said, laughing over her shoulder.

Lyra forgot her frustration. "Come on, Misty!"

They set off toward an even wider part of the stream. Lyra gripped Misty's long mane and felt her heart leap as her unicorn took off. The water sparkled beneath them for a second, and then they landed safely on the far bank.

"Our turn!" called Ivy, and Flame leaped gracefully over the water.

But Evie shook her head when it was her and Sunshine's turn. "We'll just watch." She clapped and cheered as the other three took turns jumping over wider and wider stretches.

It was a close competition. Ivy and Flame dropped out first, and after Sienna and Sparkle

had jumped a really wide part of the stream, Misty shook her head. "I can't jump that far," she told Lyra. "I'm sure of it."

"Okay. That's fine," said Lyra, not wanting to force her. "You win," she called to Sienna. "Well done. Sparkle was great."

Sienna whooped in delight. "We're the champions!" she said, punching the air. She leaned down and hugged Sparkle. He snorted happily, then jumped back over the stream to join the others.

"We should probably go back to the stables," said Evie, looking at the sun sinking in the sky.

"Yes, it'll be dark soon," said Sienna. "Come on. Last one there is a rotten egg!" She pressed her heels to Sparkle's sides.

Laughing and shouting, the others galloped after her.

After settling the unicorns with big buckets of sky berries and some hay, the girls walked back to school. The sun was setting, and the academy's tall marble-and-glass towers glowed against the red-gold sky. Lyra looked for the north tower. Ruby dorm was on the top floor of the tower, along with Topaz dorm. The setting sun made the five windows glow pink.

Lyra frowned and stopped for a moment, letting the others walk ahead. Five! That wasn't right, was it? The two dorms were identical, and they had two windows each, so why was there a fifth window above Ruby dorm?

There must be another room—a hidden room—above our dorm, she realized.

"Hey!" she called.

The others looked back.

"What's up?" asked Ivy.

"Look at our tower and count the number of windows."

They all glanced up at the tower, then turned to Lyra.

"There are five," said Sienna. "So?"

Lyra quickly explained what she'd discovered. "There must be a hidden room! I'm going to try to find it. Ruby dorm, there's a mystery we need to solve!"

CHAPTER 3

The girls stood on the circular landing at the top of the tower, looking confused. "If there is a secret room, there's no way up to it from here," said Sienna.

On one side was Ruby dorm, and on the other side was Topaz dorm, where four boys—Sam, Reuben, Archie, and Nawaz—slept.

"There isn't a hidden door anywhere out here," said Lyra, tapping the wall between the dorms.

"And we've checked our room," said Ivy. "We didn't find any hidden doors in there."

"What about in the boys' dorm?" suggested Sienna.

"We should probably ask them before we go in and look," said Evie slowly.

"If we don't touch anything, I'm sure it'll be okay," said Sienna.

Lyra nodded. "We can't give up yet. First rule of exploring: You have to take risks!" Turning the door handle, she went inside.

The boys' room was a mirror image of the girls', but it was decorated in blue and gold instead of red. There were four beds, each with a blue-and-gold blanket. There was a fluffy gold rug on the floor and blue-and-gold curtains at the windows. On the dressers beside each bed, the boys had put photos of their families and pets. They also had a shelf for their books, magazines, and school folders.

Lyra's nose wrinkled at the smell of sweaty feet

as she picked her way across the floor. A tapestry of three unicorn foals hung on the wall. Could there be a door hidden behind it? She pushed it aside. No, there was just solid wall. The girls checked every inch of the room but found nothing.

"There's no entrance here, either," said Lyra in frustration. She really wanted to solve the mystery!

"Time for a break," said Ivy, going to the door. "I vote we make hot chocolate in our lounge."

"We can't just abandon the search!" protested Lyra.

"I vote for hot chocolate too," said Sienna.

"With marshmallows," agreed Evie.

Lyra gave in and led the way down the spiral staircase. At the bottom of the stairs were two lounges, one for Topaz dorm and one for Ruby dorm. On the wall between them was a

large tapestry of a magnificent unicorn with a golden mane standing beside a forest pool. A tear trickled down the unicorn's face. Her name was embroidered at the bottom: *Daybreak*. The strange tapestry had caught Lyra's attention on their first day at the school, making her wonder who Daybreak was and why she was crying. She looked at it as she waited for Ivy and Evie to catch up. Evie had almost reached the lounge when she missed a step. She clattered down the last three stairs and landed on her bottom.

"Evie! Are you okay?" Lyra rushed to help her up.

"I'm fine." Evie turned bright red as Lyra helped her to her feet.

Lyra glanced down and noticed a tiny carving scratched into the stone on the bottom step. "It's Daybreak!" she said in surprise. "That unicorn on the tapestry over there. It's definitely her. Look at the teardrop on her face and the pool of water at her feet. But why would someone put it here?"

There was a circle around the picture, and Lyra ran a finger over it. To her surprise, the circle moved. She pressed harder. "It's a button!" she cried.

With a scraping sound, a section of the wall behind the tapestry slid back.

Sienna and Ivy squealed and raced over. Pulling aside the tapestry, they saw a second spiral staircase, smaller and darker than the one they had just come down.

"Look at that!" said Sienna in surprise.

"I knew it." Lyra could hardly breathe she was so excited. "It has to be the way up to the secret room! Come on, let's check it out."

Cobwebs hung from the staircase, and the steps were covered in a thick layer of dust. "No one's been up here in a long time," Lyra said as she climbed.

At the top was a small room with a window set in the curved wall. The stone walls and the dark wooden floorboards were empty, and the window was grimy.

Lyra looked around the gloomy room. It was really weird to think she was standing above Ruby dorm in a space that looked like it had been forgotten about years ago.

"There's nothing in here," said Sienna. "Why bother to hide a room and not put anything exciting in it?"

She and Ivy went to the window and looked out at the school grounds while Evie waited nervously in the doorway.

Lyra looked carefully around the room. When a floorboard under her foot creaked, she jumped back, thinking the wood must be rotten. She looked down at it. The floorboard seemed fine, so she kneeled to investigate. One end of the board dipped below the level of the others. Then her eyes caught sight of something strange. At the other end of the floorboard was a hinge. She almost hadn't seen it because it was made of dark metal and blended in with the wood.

"Can we go back down now?" asked Evie uneasily. "We might get into trouble."

"Wait!" said Lyra, pulling a multi-tool from her pocket. It had lots of useful tools in it, including a screwdriver. She wedged the flat end of the

24

screwdriver under the end of the floorboard and pushed it up, revealing a space underneath.

Lyra's heart beat fast. She lay down and reached into the space.

"What are you doing?" asked Sienna, coming over.

Lyra's fingers closed on a piece of paper, and she gasped. "I found something!" she said, pulling it out.

The other three crowded around her.

"What is it?" Ivy asked eagerly.

Sitting up, Lyra smoothed the paper out. It was thick and sepia-colored, the edges curling with age. There were pictures drawn in each corner in faded ink. In the center was some writing in an old-fashioned, curly script.

"It's just some scrap paper," said Sienna, disappointed.

"But why would someone hide an old scrap of paper?" asked Evie.

Sienna shrugged. "It probably just fell under the floorboard and—"

"No, wait!" Lyra looked up, her eyes bright with excitement. "I think it's a treasure map!"

CHAPTER 4

"A treasure map?" breathed Sienna. "For real?"

"Yes! Look!" Lyra pointed to the top right-hand corner. "That's a picture of the school with Sparkle Lake and here"—she pointed to the bottom left-hand corner—"is a tower."

"And the bit in that corner," added Evie, "looks like a maze. That mark right at the very edge could be part of an X!"

Sienna gasped. "X marks the spot! Oh wow! It really could be a treasure map!"

"What does the writing say, Lyra?" asked Evie eagerly.

Lyra looked closely. The letters were faint, and the handwriting was hard to read. There were four lines. "It's just a list of random things." She read them out loud: *"The Northernmost Door. The Phoenix's Claw. The Salamander's Stare. The Dragon's Lair."*

"What does it all mean?" Sienna asked.

"I have no idea, but I'm sure if we can figure them out, we'll find the treasure—whatever it is!" Lyra said excitedly.

"Wait." Evie took the paper from Lyra and studied it carefully. "I think this is just one *part* of a treasure map. Look, the two edges on the inside are sharper, like they were cut by scissors. The picture of the school isn't a complete picture; it's been cut in half. The tower and maze too. I think this is just a piece of the map."

"So where's the rest?" asked Sienna.

"Maybe there's more in the hole," said Ivy.

Lyra lay down on her stomach again and felt around, but there wasn't anything else under the floorboard. "No, nothing there," she said. But as she sat up, she saw the underside of the piece of paper in Evie's hands.

"There's more writing on the other side!" she exclaimed.

Evie turned the paper over. "This writing is newer; it's not so faded. Listen!

"Go to the woods for what you seek.

Find Daybreak, move stone, follow river deep.

Where spiders live and a cave answers your call,

The piece lies behind a glittering wall."

"It's a riddle," said Ivy.

"It's not just a riddle," said Lyra, taking the piece of the map from her. "It's a clue! A clue that will lead us to another piece of the map."

"But why would someone cut up a map and hide the pieces?" wondered Evie.

"I have no idea," said Lyra. Her eyes shone with determination. "But this is a mystery we are going to solve."

Just then, there was the sound of a distant gong ringing.

"It's dinnertime!" said Sienna. "We'd better hurry up. We don't want to miss it."

"Definitely not!" agreed Lyra. After dinner, Dr. Briar, a famous archaeologist, was going to be giving a talk to the students. Lyra couldn't wait.

They hurried back down the staircase and out from behind the tapestry. Lyra had just pressed the button to close the secret entrance when the four boys from Topaz dorm came down the stairs.

"What have you been doing?" said Sam, who was tall with wavy blond hair. He looked down his nose at Lyra.

"Taking a dust bath?" said Archie with a grin.

"Or cuddling spiders? You've all got cobwebs in your hair," said Reuben.

Lyra shrugged. "We've just been messing around," she said.

"How about you?" asked Sienna, quickly changing the subject. "What have you been up to?"

"We've been practicing crossnet all afternoon," said Archie as they set off to the dining hall together. "We're definitely going to win the inter-dorm tournament tomorrow." Crossnet was a game played on unicorns. Each player had a stick with a net at the top, and they had to pass a ball from player to player, scoring points by throwing the ball through the goal at the end of the field. It was fast and furious and lots of fun!

"Boys are the best," chanted Nawaz.

"In your dreams!" Sienna said. "We'll beat you tomorrow."

"I don't think so—" said Reuben.

"What's that?" Sam interrupted, pointing to the piece of map that Lyra was holding.

"Nothing," she said quickly. "Just a bit of paper I picked up."

"It looks really old," said Sam, stepping closer.

"Yeah, well, I'm into history and old stuff," said Lyra, putting it into her pocket.

"You should show it to my aunt. She might be able to tell you more about it," said Sam.

"Your aunt?"

"Don't you know? My aunt is Dr. Angelica Briar, the archaeologist who's giving the talk after dinner."

"Your aunt is Dr. Briar!" Lyra exclaimed.

"Yes." Sam was almost bursting with smugness.

"I've been on digs with her before, and I'll be helping with her talk tonight."

Lyra felt a flash of jealousy. "Oh."

They reached the dining hall, a long room with windows overlooking the lake. It was lit by hundreds of tiny white lights that sparkled against the dark sky.

"Enjoy the talk," Sam said to Lyra. "If you're lucky, my aunt might even give you her autograph." He grinned and walked away.

Lyra scowled after him, then spotted an elegant woman with shoulder-length dark hair, who was sitting at the head table with the teachers. Her hair was held back with a jeweled clip, and she had rings on all her fingers. She was talking to Ms. Nettles. *Dr. Briar!* Lyra thought with excitement. She recognized her from magazine articles she had read.

"Hey, do you think Sam's right? Should we

show Dr. Briar the piece of the map after the talk?" she asked, nudging the others.

"Good plan," said Ivy.

Sienna and Evie nodded.

Lyra crossed her fingers. Would Dr. Briar be able to make sense of the words on the map? She really hoped so!

Dinner was delicious: veggie burgers with sweet potato fries and salad followed by gooey chocolate brownies and ice cream. When it was over, the tables were cleared, and Sam helped Dr. Briar lay out ancient artifacts. Lyra felt a pang of envy as she watched.

"Why are they wearing gloves?" asked Ivy, peering over Lyra's shoulder.

"Because the oils in your hand can damage anything old," Lyra explained.

"I hope this talk isn't going to be boring," muttered Sienna.

35

"It won't be!" said Lyra.

She was right. When Dr. Briar began her talk, it quickly became clear that she had a wonderful way of bringing history to life. She told the students fascinating stories of how people had once lived and how they had used the objects. To Lyra's surprise, Sam chimed in at times and seemed just as excited as his aunt. He seemed to be really into history and archaeology. He brought out some of the ancient pots, tools, and jewelry for everyone to look at.

At the end of the talk, as the students left, Ruby dorm stayed.

Dr. Briar smiled at them. "Hello, girls. Do you have a question?"

Lyra took the map out of her pocket. "We found this earlier. It has writing and pictures on it. We wondered if you might know what they mean."

Dr. Briar's eyes twinkled. "Let's have a look. Maybe you've stumbled on some great find."

Lyra blushed as she handed the map over. What if they were wrong and it was just a bit of scrap paper after all?

Dr. Briar studied it carefully, her smile changing to a frown of concentration as she turned

it this way and that. Lyra held her breath. Dr. Briar's eyes were focused. That had to be a good sign, right?

At last, Dr. Briar looked up at them. "Well, it's rather fun," she said lightly. "One of my friends who collects old manuscripts would probably love to see it, but I'm sorry to say that it's not of any value."

"Oh!" said Sienna. "So it's not part of a treasure map?"

"A treasure map?" Dr. Briar laughed. "Oh no, girls. I'd guess it's about a hundred years old, but it's just some random scribblings."

Lyra felt confused. She'd seen how carefully Dr. Briar had studied the map. If it was worthless, why had she looked at it for so long?

"Where did you find it?" Dr. Briar asked.

"In a—" Sienna began.

Lyra suddenly felt that she didn't want to tell

Dr. Briar about the secret room. "In a room somewhere in school," she finished.

"Well, like I said, I'm sure one of my friends who collects old manuscripts would like to have it, just out of curiosity," said Dr. Briar. "I'll pass it on if you like."

"No," said Lyra quickly, grabbing the paper before Dr. Briar could pocket it. "I want to keep it."

Dr. Briar frowned. "Are you sure?" She held on to the paper.

"Yes, definitely," said Lyra. "I like old things." She watched Dr. Briar's face. "That's not a problem, is it? You said it's not valuable."

"Of course not." Dr. Briar smiled as she let the paper go. "If you change your mind, just ask Sam to let me know. Which dorm are you, by the way?"

"Ruby," said Evie.

"Great, well, nice meeting you, girls. I'd better finish up here. If you see Sam, could you ask him to come have a quick chat with me?" Then Dr. Briar turned away.

Lyra felt disappointed and confused as they left the dining hall. A worried thought crossed her mind. Had Dr. Briar been lying? But what possible reason could she have for misleading them?

No matter what she says, I'm sure it's part of a treasure map, thought Lyra.

Feeling happy she still had the paper, she followed the others out of the dining hall.

CHAPTER 5

The next day, the inter-dorm crossnet tournament was planned for the afternoon, but first Ruby and Topaz dorms had a Geography and Culture class. Lyra's dreams had been full of treasure maps and mysterious clues. While Ms. Rivers talked about ecosystems, Lyra thought about the riddle on the back of the map. She repeated the words in her head.

Go to the woods for what you seek.
Find Daybreak, move stone, follow river deep.
Where spiders live and a cave answers your call,
The piece lies behind a glittering wall.

She frowned. What did it all mean?

"Lyra?"

Lyra jumped as she realized Ms. Rivers and the whole class were staring at her.

"S-sorry," she said. "Can you repeat the question?"

Sam snickered, but Ivy sent her a kind smile.

Ms. Rivers sighed. "Can you give me an example of an animal that lives in the woods?"

Across the room, Evie flapped her arms behind Ms. Rivers.

"Birds," said Lyra.

Ms. Rivers looked unimpressed. "Yes, Lyra, there are birds in the woods. I was hoping you could name one."

"Um . . ."

Evie pulled at her nose and wiggled her fingers like spiders.

"The stretchy-nosed spidery bird?" guessed Lyra.

Ms. Rivers's eyebrows almost hit her hairline as the rest of the class giggled.

"Ms. Rivers, I think Lyra is talking about the long-beaked spider crow," Sam said.

"Thank you, Sam," said Ms. Rivers. "You are correct. Long-beaked spider crows roost near the Echo Caves at the edge of the woods and feed on cave spiders." She glared at Lyra. "Please pay attention, Lyra."

Lyra blushed and sank down in her seat.

"Who can name any animals that live in the caves?" Ms. Rivers asked.

As she moved on, choosing people to answer, something in Lyra's brain clicked. She only just

managed to stop herself from gasping out loud. *Cave spiders! Echo Caves!* The words of the riddle ran through her head again: *Where spiders live and a cave answers your call.* An echo made it sound like a voice was answering you, and there were spiders in the Echo Caves. Maybe the map was hidden there!

She glanced over at Ivy, Sienna, and Evie. She wanted to share her discovery! But as Ms. Rivers turned to her, she forced herself to pay attention and listen.

At the end of class, Lyra hurried everyone up to their dorm. Shutting the door behind her, she faced her friends.

"I've done it! I've solved the clue. We need to go to the Echo Caves!" She raced through her explanation.

"I bet you're right," said Evie in excitement. "How about we go there this afternoon?"

"But what about the crossnet tournament?" protested Sienna.

Lyra bit her lip. She wanted to play in the tournament, but following the clue was definitely more important. "We can miss it. The teachers said it wasn't required."

"But I want to play," said Sienna, frowning.

"More than you want to find treasure?" asked Lyra.

Sienna hesitated. "I guess I'd rather find another part of the map."

Lyra grinned. "Great! So this afternoon we'll go map hunting!"

After lunch, they went to the stables and told the unicorns their plan. Lyra had a backpack

with her—it was her explorer's bag. It had things that might be useful, like string, her multi-tool, a first aid kit, flashlights, snacks, and some extra clothes. *Be adventure-ready.* That was her motto.

She had memorized a map of the school grounds, so she and Misty led the way out through the meadow. They followed the stream, then went to the left and up a steep hill. At the top, the unicorns stopped. They looked down at

the woods spread out beneath them. The trees were tall and scary-looking.

"You know we're not allowed in those woods," said Misty uneasily.

"We don't have to go all the way in," said Lyra. "The caves are near the edge."

They rode down the hill, the unicorns' hooves slipping on loose rocks. Through the trees they could just make out the caves. One was much larger than the rest, and a thick curtain of vines hung down over its opening.

Misty stopped suddenly. Lyra patted her neck, encouraging her to go on, but she didn't move.

"What's up?" Lyra could barely hide her impatience.

"I heard a noise." Misty looked around, then snorted and jumped backward. "Up there! There's something watching from that tree!"

Goose bumps shivered up Lyra's arms, and she gripped Misty's mane tightly. Something with a sharp hooked nose peered down at them from between the branches. Lyra tried to tell the others, but her mouth was too dry to speak. Sienna and Sparkle rode on, Sparkle's hooves crunching as he stepped on a stick.

There was a startled squawk and a whoosh of air. A huge bird flew out of the tree, its blue-black wings flapping wildly. Lyra burst out laughing. "It was only a bird, Misty! A long-beaked spider crow! That means we're definitely in the right place."

By now Sienna and Sparkle had reached the curtain of vines. Sienna pulled it back. "Should I lead the way?" she said, peering into the darkness.

No! thought Lyra. She wanted to go first!

But it was too late. Sienna and Sparkle were already entering the cave. The others followed. Only Misty remained outside.

"What are you doing, Misty?" said Lyra impatiently. "We need to catch up with the others!"

"I don't want to go in," said Misty. "It could be dangerous!"

"What can you see?" Lyra called to her friends.

"It's empty." Sienna's voice echoed back at her. "But there's a tunnel at the back."

"The next piece of the map might be hidden in the tunnel," said Ivy, her voice echoing too.

Lyra dismounted. She had to see this for herself. "Wait up! Don't go any farther without me!"

Misty stamped her hoof on the ground as Lyra started toward the cave. "Lyra, come back!"

For a second, Lyra saw something sparkling in the air—but then it was gone. A smell blew by,

sweet like cotton candy. It reminded her of something, but there wasn't time to think about it. She wanted to see the tunnel! "It'll be fine, Misty. Please come with me."

"I don't want to," said Misty.

Lyra gave up trying to convince her. So instead she pulled her flashlight out and walked into the cave. The light picked out the cobwebs hanging from the ceiling. Large, friendly cave spiders with googly eyes and fluffy legs watched the girls curiously. Lyra headed for the tunnel where her friends were standing with their unicorns. There was a pile of dirt and stones at the entrance.

"It looks like part of the ceiling's come down," said Evie.

"We can still get through, though." Lyra scrambled over the heap of rubble. "The tunnel clears when you get past this bit. It's wide enough for us to ride through." She turned. "Come on!" she called to Misty.

"Yes, don't be a spoilsport, Misty," said Sienna. "Come and join us."

Flame, Ivy's unicorn, stamped a hoof. "Don't you want to have an adventure?"

"No," Misty called back firmly.

Lyra's flashlight beam fell on a small picture carved into the stone wall of the tunnel. "There's a tiny unicorn carved into the rock. It has a teardrop on its face. It's Daybreak!" Lyra's eyes glowed.

"Oh wow. This must mean we have to go down the tunnel. The clue said *Find Daybreak*. Remember?"

The others nodded.

"I'm going on. Who's with me?" asked Lyra.

"Me!" cried everyone except Misty.

"Misty?" Lyra asked, scrambling back over the rubble.

"I guess so," Misty muttered.

Lyra was relieved. She didn't want to have an argument with Misty in front of everyone. She ran to Misty and jumped on her back. They rode into the cave together. Misty stepped carefully over the rubble, her hooves slipping and sliding. "Follow us, everyone," Lyra said in excitement, "and keep your eyes open for the next piece of the map!"

CHAPTER 6

The tunnel sloped downward. Moss clung to the walls, and the unicorns' hooves clattered on the stony floor. After they had been riding for a while, the ground flattened out. There were lots of other tunnels, but there was a little stone carving of Daybreak that showed them which way to go. Lyra was so excited! Were they really about to find another piece of the treasure map?

"Is that water?" asked Sienna as they heard a tinkly sound in the distance.

"It can't be. We're underground," said Ivy.

"Rivers and streams can run underground," said Evie as they rode on.

"Oh wow!" Lyra breathed as they rounded another corner. The tunnel opened into a huge cavern. Its high ceiling arched above them, and

a glittering rainbow-colored river flowed through it. The rocky walls glowed with a strange shimmering light. Gold-striped fish jumped in and out of the water while huge dragonflies with green iridescent wings darted above them.

"Which way do we go?" said Ivy, looking up and down the river.

"Here's another picture," Sienna said excitedly. She pointed at a boulder to the right. Sure enough, the boulder was marked with a tiny Daybreak.

They rode beside the river, following the carvings until a wall of rock rose up in front of them and the river disappeared into a narrow hole. There was no way they could follow it. To their right were two tunnels.

"Which one should we take?" Lyra shone her flashlight into each of them, looking for another tiny picture of a unicorn, but she couldn't find one anywhere.

"That tunnel looks bigger. I bet it's this way," cried Sienna, riding past Lyra and Misty.

Evie and Sunshine and Ivy and Flame followed her. Lyra felt a flicker of annoyance. This was her expedition, not Sienna's! "Hurry up, we're getting left behind," she said to Misty, who was stepping very carefully over the uneven floor.

The tunnel twisted and turned until they saw a circle of light ahead.

"That must be the way out," said Evie.

"But we still haven't found the map," protested Lyra.

The others seemed more interested in seeing where they were going to come out.

"I bet we're in the mountains," said Sienna.

"Or we've walked in a circle and we're back in the woods," said Evie.

Lyra switched off her flashlight as they

emerged into the daylight. There was an old brick shed in front of them with a compost heap and a willow tree beside it.

"Where are we?" asked Sienna.

"We're in the vegetable garden," said Lyra. She rode Misty around the shed and saw the school gardens spread out in front of her.

"Look," whispered Evie, who had followed her. "Sam and Flash are over there. It looks like they're cooling off after the crossnet tournament."

"I wonder which dorm won," said Sienna. "I hope it wasn't Topaz or we'll never hear the end of it."

"Don't let Sam see us," said Lyra. "He'll want to know what we've been doing."

They ducked behind the shed and waited for Sam and Flash to leave before they headed back to the stables. On their way, they saw a group of

students from Sapphire dorm gathered around a unicorn with a bright orange-and-gold mane.

"What's going on?" asked Ivy.

Lexi and Katy, two of the girls in Sapphire dorm, saw them and waved. "Come and watch!" Lexi called. "Elise and Peony have just discovered Peony's magic. They're first in the year."

"What can Peony do?" Lyra asked eagerly.

Elise, a tall girl with curly red hair, beamed. "She's got summoning magic." She put her hand on her unicorn's neck. "Peony, will you please get my hoodie from the stables?"

Peony stamped a hoof. Blue sparkles flew up and a sweet smell of burnt sugar filled the air. A few seconds later, a blue hoodie came flying toward them. She snorted in surprise as it landed on her head.

Elise giggled. "We still have some prac-

ticing to do, but isn't it amazing?" She hugged Peony, who nuzzled her.

"It's awesome!" said Lyra. She was happy for Elise and Peony, but also felt a flash of jealousy. Elise was so lucky! When would Misty discover her magic?

"How did you discover it?" asked Sienna, who also looked a bit jealous.

"It was when we were playing crossnet," said Elise. "The ball just kept flying out of other people's nets into mine!"

"We were about to win the match twenty goals to one," said Lexi, "but then Ms. Nettles realized

what was going on and she gave the match to Topaz dorm."

"Who won the tournament overall?" asked Ivy.

"Topaz," said Katy.

Sienna groaned.

Elise gave them a curious look. "Where were you?"

"We had something else to do," Lyra said.

Katy grinned. "The Topaz boys said you were scared they'd beat you!"

"As if!" said Sienna. "I can't believe it," she said grumpily as they rode away. "Now the boys think we were too chicken to play against them. If we'd been playing crossnet, we might have won the tournament and maybe one of our unicorns would have discovered *their* magic. Instead we just got to ride down lots of tunnels and found nothing at all."

"We must have taken a wrong turn some-

60

where," said Lyra. "We should go back and try again. There's just enough time before dinner. . . ."

The others shook their heads.

"No, not now. The unicorns are tired," said Evie.

"And I'm hungry," said Ivy.

"But—" Lyra began.

"Wherever the map is hidden, it's safe, Lyra," Ivy said.

Sienna nodded. "Ivy's right. We can try again tomorrow or this weekend."

Lyra sighed. She knew the others were right, but she wanted to find the map *now*!

CHAPTER 7

Back in the stables, Lyra brushed Misty and got her some sky berries. "I wish we'd found another piece of the map," she said.

"Mmm," said Misty. She gave a shiver. "I didn't like those caves very much."

"They were fine," said Lyra. "There wasn't anything to be scared of."

Misty sighed. "When I was little I found everything scary. My older sister, Dewdrop, used to tease me and say I was scared of my own shadow. She's always been much braver than me." She

snorted sadly. "I do miss her. I bet you'd like her, Lyra. She's—"

"Hey," Lyra interrupted. She didn't want Misty to start feeling sad about missing her family. "I've just had an idea. Maybe I can persuade the others to go back to the caves tomorrow morning. Ms. Rivers has organized a treasure hunt. It's supposed to help us learn more about the school and the grounds, but I bet we could sneak off and no one would notice. What do you think?"

"You could try," Misty muttered.

"I will!" said Lyra. "A treasure hunt is fun, but finding another piece of a real treasure map will be even better! See you later, Misty."

She left the stables and caught up with her friends as they reached the school building. "How about this for a plan?" Lyra said as they went up the staircase to Ruby dorm. "Instead of doing

the treasure hunt tomorrow, we—" She broke off with a gasp as Sienna opened the door to their dorm.

Their room had been completely ransacked! Clothes spilled from open drawers, and the floor was covered with books, pencils, and papers.

"What's happened?" asked Evie, her eyes huge.

Lyra and the others picked their way through the mess to their beds.

"None of my things are missing," said Lyra in relief.

"Same," said Ivy and Evie.

"All my stuff is here." Sienna put her hands on her hips. "So who did this?"

"And why?" added Evie.

Lyra touched the map piece in her pocket. Could someone have been looking for it? The only other people who knew about it were Dr. Briar and Sam, and Dr. Briar wasn't at the school anymore. *Sam is, though,* she thought.

"I bet it was the Topaz boys," said Sienna, picking a hoodie up from the floor. "They must have realized we'd been in their dorm yesterday and decided to get back at us."

"But why make such a mess?" said Ivy, looking around. "We didn't wreck their room."

"Maybe they thought it was funny," said Sienna.

"No, they're not that mean," said Evie.

"It could have been just Sam, not all the boys," said Lyra. "If Dr. Briar didn't tell us the truth, and the map is valuable, then she might have asked Sam to try to find it."

"But she said it wasn't worth anything. Why would she lie?" asked Evie.

"Maybe because it's *really* valuable. So valuable she didn't want us to realize what we had," said Lyra.

Her friends didn't look convinced.

Sienna shook her head. "I still think it was the boys just trying to annoy us."

"We don't know that," Lyra insisted. "We have to find the rest of the map in case Dr. Briar is looking for it too. Let's go tomorrow morning when everyone else is doing the treasure hunt."

"But we already missed the crossnet match, and I want to do the treasure hunt!" protested Sienna.

"Me too," said Evie. "Ms. Rivers said it would help us to learn more about the school."

"Tomorrow's our last chance. If we don't go then, we'll have to wait until the weekend," Lyra said impatiently.

"The map can wait," said Sienna, shrugging.

Evie nodded. "I agree with Sienna."

"Me too," said Ivy.

"Three votes to one," Sienna told Lyra.

Lyra stared at them. She couldn't believe they would rather do a fake treasure hunt than look for the map and some real treasure. But the others had voted against her. Feeling frustrated, she put away her things, shoved her clothes into her drawers, and yanked the covers straight on her bed.

She was still feeling upset when it was time to settle the unicorns for the night. She made an excuse so the others would go to the stables

without her, and then she stomped after them alone.

Misty whinnied when she saw her. "I thought you weren't coming."

"Sorry," muttered Lyra grumpily. She emptied a bucket of sky berries into the unicorn's manger.

Misty nuzzled her. "Are you okay?"

"Mmm," said Lyra.

"Is this about you wanting to miss the treasure hunt to go look for the map?" Misty asked. "I heard Sienna telling Sparkle about it."

"The map piece must be important for Sam to go through our things," said Lyra. "There's no time to lose. We should continue our search tomorrow." She added, "I think I'll go on my own. Will you come with me?"

Misty looked alarmed. "But what if the teachers find out and we get into trouble?"

Lyra shrugged. "Hopefully they won't."

"Lyra, I don't think you should do this."

Lyra felt a sharp stab of frustration. "Oh, Misty!" she snapped. "Why do you always have to be so boring?"

Misty's eyes widened with hurt, and Lyra instantly felt awful. "Sorry, I didn't mean it," she said quickly as Misty hung her head.

"I really didn't," said Lyra, but Misty just continued to stare at the floor.

Just then, Evie looked over the door. "There

you are, Lyra. Are you coming? We need to get back before the bedtime bell."

Lyra hesitated. She didn't want to leave Misty when she'd hurt her feelings, but the teachers were very strict about everyone being back in their dorm on time. She gave Misty a quick hug. "Goodnight," she said, but Misty didn't reply.

Lyra walked back to the dorm feeling very guilty. She shouldn't have snapped at Misty. She was upset, but it wasn't fair to take it out on her sweet-natured unicorn.

"Are you okay?" Evie asked as they got into their pajamas. "You've been really quiet this evening."

"I have a headache," Lyra lied.

She pulled the soft, feather-filled blanket over her head, regret coursing through her. *I'll make it up to Misty first thing in the morning,* she promised herself.

CHAPTER 8

The others quickly fell asleep, but Lyra tossed and turned, her thoughts jumping between Misty and the treasure map. The night felt like it was going on forever. At five o'clock she sat up and looked through the window at the stars twinkling in the sky. A full moon was shining down. *I can't stay in bed any longer,* she thought. *I have to see Misty and say I'm sorry.* She quietly pulled on her riding pants and jacket and crept out of the dorm.

The early-morning air was icy cold, and her breath froze in white clouds as she ran across the grass toward the stables. As she got closer, she

paused. A unicorn with a long purple-and-green mane was creeping through the stable yard.

"Misty!" Lyra exclaimed. "Where are you going?"

Misty jumped. "Lyra!"

"What's going on?" Lyra ran over, her feet crunching on the grass.

Misty hung her head and mumbled, "I . . . I'm going home."

"Going home?" Lyra stared at her. "What do you mean?"

Misty gulped. "I'm missing my family, and, well . . . I think you'd be happier if you were paired with another unicorn. Someone brave and adventurous, like you."

Lyra stared at her. "But I don't want any other unicorn. I want you. You're perfect for me."

Misty shook her head. "I'm not. I'm boring."

She heaved a sigh. "Don't try to stop me, Lyra. It's best if I just go home."

Lyra planted herself in front of her unicorn. "Stop right there. You're not going anywhere, Misty," she said. "I don't want another unicorn, and I'm really sorry about what I said yesterday.

I was angry and I took it out on you, and that was wrong. You're not boring. You're wonderful, and I love you!"

Misty looked at her through her long eyelashes. "Really?" she said tentatively.

"Really," Lyra told her. She put her arms around Misty's neck. "Will you please stay?"

Misty rested her face against Lyra's chest and gave a deep, happy sigh. "Yes," she breathed.

Lyra felt a rush of relief. "Thank you. I really couldn't bear it if you left. I'm so sorry you're feeling homesick." She stroked Misty's silky mane. "You told me you were missing your family, and I should have listened. Is there anything I can do to help?"

"Just knowing you want me to stay helps," said Misty softly. "I do miss my family, but I won't miss them quite so much now I'm sure that you really want me to be your unicorn."

"I really do, and anytime you want to talk about your family, I promise I'll listen," said Lyra. She kissed Misty's forehead. "I can't wait to meet them. And for you to meet my family too."

They stood there for a moment until Lyra realized that her toes and fingers were turning to ice. "We'd better go inside. It's freezing out here."

They walked back to the stables, Lyra's arm over Misty's neck.

Misty glanced at the still-dark sky. "Why are you up so early?" she asked.

"I couldn't sleep. I was thinking about you and wanting to say sorry and also thinking about the treasure map. I have to search those caves again in case we missed something, but the others want to wait until the weekend." Lyra sighed. "I know it's only a few more days, but yesterday our dorm was ransacked. I'm worried that someone else is also after the map."

Misty stopped. "Then let's go now."

Lyra frowned. "What?"

"To the caves. You and me," said Misty, nuzzling her. "If you really want to go back there, then I'll come with you."

"Really? Let's do it! If we're quick, we might even be back in time for the treasure hunt. I need to get my explorer's bag first, though. You know, the one with all my useful stuff, like flashlights, a compass, supplies—"

"Go get it," Misty interrupted. "Hurry!"

A smile lit up Lyra's face. "Misty, you're the best!" Lyra hugged her, then raced back to her dorm.

Sienna, Evie, and Ivy were still fast asleep as Lyra tiptoed in and took her backpack from under her bed. But Evie, in the bed next to her, stirred as she picked it up.

"Lyra?"

Lyra froze.

Evie propped herself up, blinking at Lyra through the dark. "What are you doing?"

"Nothing," Lyra whispered. "Go back to sleep."

Evie nodded and curled up under her blanket.

With her heart beating at double speed, Lyra crept out of the dorm.

She raced across the grass to where Misty was waiting. "Got it!" she whispered, holding up her bag. She climbed onto Misty's back. "Let's go!"

CHAPTER 9

Lyra and Misty had just reached the entrance to the tunnel in the rose garden when they heard the sound of hooves. Lyra swung around and saw the rest of Ruby dorm galloping across the moonlit grass toward them.

"There they are!"

"Lyra! Misty! Wait!"

Sienna and Sparkle reached them first. "What are you doing?" Sienna demanded as Sparkle came to a halt.

"I was about to go back to sleep when I realized you were fully dressed and that you had your

78

explorer's bag," said Evie, catching up, "so I woke the others."

"We went to the stables and saw that Misty was gone," Sienna continued. "Then we spotted some hoofprints on the frosty grass, so we followed them."

"And now we've found you!" finished Ivy. "You were about to go hunting for the map without us, weren't you?"

Sienna grinned. "Well, it doesn't matter because now we're coming along too. An early-morning adventure, how awesome is that?"

Lyra felt her heart lift. "Very awesome!" she said, grinning back. "But first we need to be prepared." She rummaged around in her bag and handed out flashlights. "Everyone ready?" They all nodded. "Then follow me!"

Lyra and Misty led the way into the tunnel, crossing the uneven ground until they came out

into the cavern where the sparkling river disappeared through the rocky wall.

"We didn't find the map in this tunnel, so it must be in that one!" said Sienna, pointing to the smaller tunnel that they hadn't taken.

"Are you sure? It doesn't have a picture of Daybreak, either," Lyra said. "I think we should go back to the last carving we found."

"Lyra's right," said Misty. "If the pictures have led us this far, it doesn't seem right that they suddenly disappear. Let's go back to the last one and look around."

Lyra felt a rush of gratitude to Misty for backing her up. She stroked her neck. "Thanks," she whispered as they retraced their steps. Misty snorted happily, and for the first time Lyra felt like they were a real team.

When they got back to the last picture of

Daybreak, there was only one way to go. Lyra thought that was strange. All the other carvings had been at tunnel crossings where they had to make decisions. Her mind whirred as she studied it. There was a faint circle surrounding it, identical to the one around the picture on the stair back in their tower.

Holding her breath, Lyra leaned down from Misty's back and pressed it hard. Would it work?

The carving moved under her fingers, followed by a loud scraping noise. Everyone cried out as a section of the rocky wall at the end of the cavern slid to the side. Through the gap they could see the river widening out and flowing on through more caves.

"That must be where we have to go!" cried Lyra. "Remember the clue: *Find Daybreak, move stone, follow river deep!*"

Evie nodded. "*Find Daybreak, move stone* must have meant pressing the button."

"So now we follow the deep river," said Lyra.

Misty trotted to the gap. From there, Lyra saw that the river had a wide bank on both sides. There was a large wooden raft tied to a rock, which was bobbing gently on the moving water. "A raft! Let's use it to float down the river."

"Awesome!" said Sienna.

They all clambered through the opening. "Oh wow, I've never been on a raft before," said Evie, sliding off Sunshine and scrambling across the bank toward the rafts. She reached out to pull it closer, but she lost her balance and fell into the water with a splash. She yelled as the current started to carry her down the river. Sunshine whinnied in alarm and raced to the water.

"Evie!" Sienna yelled, jumping off Sparkle.

She ran to the edge of the bank and reached out her hand. "Evie, grab my hand!"

Lyra leaped off Misty and raced over, holding her hand out as well. If they could just grab Evie as she came past . . .

"Be careful, Lyra!" Misty whinnied, stamping her hooves in worry. Purple sparks suddenly swirled into the air along with the sweet smell of burnt sugar. Glancing around, Lyra saw Misty surrounded by a swirl of iridescent purple bubbles. One bubble swelled as it floated toward the river, shimmering as it grew. It landed on the water, where it seemed to dissolve and re-form around Evie.

Lyra watched in amazement as the bubble carried Evie safely to dry land before bursting. Thousands of tiny, shiny bubbles floated away overhead.

"Wh-what just happened?" Lyra stammered as Sunshine started nuzzling Evie.

"Misty's found her magic!" cried Sienna, thumping Lyra on the back.

"Oh, well done, Misty!" cried Ivy, and all the unicorns whinnied in delight.

"Th-thank you, Misty!" stammered Evie, her teeth chattering. She was soaked, and it was cold in the caverns. "I'm so sorry, everyone!"

Lyra stared at Misty in awe. "You got your magic."

"Bubble magic—just like my mom," said Misty, looking delighted. "It means that I can protect things, make objects float in the air, and even make bubble bridges. There are all sorts of things

I'll be able to do once I've learned to control it," she added.

"It's amazing magic!" said Ivy.

Lyra threw her arms around Misty's neck, happiness shooting through her. Misty had found her magic!

"Three cheers for Misty," said Sienna. "You found your magic at just the right time."

"Yes, thanks again, Misty," said Evie.

"We'd better go back and get you dried off," said Ivy, taking in Evie's dripping clothes and chattering teeth.

"But what about the map?" Lyra said. "We've come this far. We can't go back now."

"Evie will catch a cold if she stays in her wet clothes," said Sunshine, breathing warm air on Evie's face.

Lyra felt bad. She didn't want Evie to get sick, but they were so close to discovering the next clue.

Suddenly she had an idea. Rummaging in her backpack, she pulled out a shiny silver blanket and handed it to Evie. "Here, put this around yourself. It's a survival blanket. It's really light, but it will keep you warm. I've also got extra gloves, socks, and a jacket," she said, digging them out. "But if you still want to go back to school, that's fine."

Evie pulled the clothes on and wrapped the blanket around her, snuggling down inside it. "I want to go on," she said bravely.

"Really? You're amazing! Everyone onto the raft, then!" Lyra declared.

"What about us?" said Misty. She looked doubtfully at her hooves. "I don't think unicorns and rafts mix."

"We can't leave you behind," said Lyra.

Misty snorted and tossed her mane. Finding her magic seemed to have given her new confidence. "Of course not, and we wouldn't let you go

without us. How about we pull the raft? It has two ropes. If we pair up and hold on to the ropes, we can stop the raft from going too fast if the current gets too strong."

Lyra nodded. "Good plan. Let's go."

Misty and Flame held the front rope in their mouths while Sunshine and Sparkle held the back one. There were paddles on the raft. Lyra and Sienna sat near the edges, dipping them into the water, and the unicorns helped to pull the girls along. At times the rocky ceiling soared high above them, while sometimes it was so low they had to duck. Lyra's eyes darted everywhere as they floated down the river. The second piece of the map had to be hidden here somewhere, but where? The clue said it was behind a glittering wall. She scanned the rocky sides of the caverns, but none of them glittered.

After they'd been traveling for a while, Misty turned to Lyra. "The river's starting to flow faster now," she said, looking anxious. "And I can hear a strange thundering sound in the distance. Maybe you should get off the raft?"

"No way!" said Lyra. She'd also noticed the current was getting stronger. The raft was bobbing up and down more, and she could see that the unicorns were struggling to hold on to it. But they couldn't give up. They had to find the glittering wall. She looked at the others. "Does anyone else want to get off?"

Sienna shook her head emphatically. "Nope."

"Not yet," said Ivy and Evie.

Lyra grinned at her friends. "That's settled, then. Let's keep going."

Misty's face tightened with worry.

"This is awesome!" called Sienna as the river

started to flow even faster. The front of the raft began to jump and dip in the water.

Evie gasped and hung on tightly. "It's getting very bouncy!"

"Lyra, I really think we should turn back now!" Misty had to shout to make herself heard over the rushing river.

"Not yet!" Water ran down Lyra's hair and face.

Evie and Ivy squealed as the front of the raft lifted out of the water then crashed back down.

The raft went around a bend in the river, and it was then that Lyra saw something that made her heart skip a beat. In front of them was a waterfall.

"We need to get off the raft!" she shrieked. "Everyone paddle to the bank. NOW!"

The unicorns snorted and pulled at the ropes

with all their might, their hooves slipping on the wet rock. But the current was too strong. The ropes were pulled from the unicorns' mouths, and suddenly the girls found themselves speeding straight toward the top of the waterfall.

I should have listened to Misty and turned back when she said! thought Lyra as she clung to the raft.

Her friends were shouting and screaming. The unicorns were all whinnying desperately. But there was no stopping the raft. It sped up and shot over the edge of the waterfall.

This is it, Lyra thought, shutting her eyes as she started to fall.

CHAPTER 10

Lyra tumbled through the air, surrounded by the roar of the water, but all of a sudden the noise faded. She blinked as she realized she wasn't falling but floating. Floating! A shimmering wall curved all around her. *Misty's bubble magic!*

Lyra leaped to her feet and gazed through the bubble that was carrying her safely down the waterfall. Relief rushed through her as she saw that her friends were also in giant bubbles.

They landed at the bottom, and the bubbles bounced them lightly over the surface of the river, coming to rest on the bank. Sparkle, Sunshine,

and Flame came galloping down the steep path at the side of the waterfall. Misty followed far more slowly, her sides heaving.

Lyra scrambled to her feet. Her legs felt wobbly, but she ran up the path toward Misty.

"Misty! You saved us all! I'm so sorry that I didn't listen to you. Are you okay?"

"Yes. Just tired," Misty panted. "That took a lot of magic."

"I have sky berries," said Lyra, pulling some out of her backpack that was still on her back. "Here." She fed them to Misty, stroking her all the while.

Misty started to look better. "Sky berries were

just what I needed. You always think of every-thing," she said.

"Except danger," said Lyra. "Oh, Misty, I'm so sorry. I promise I'll listen to you more in the future and try not to get us into such dangerous situations."

Misty nuzzled her. "But getting into dangerous situations isn't all bad. If we hadn't come into these caves, I might never have found my magic. And now that you're all safe, I have kind of enjoyed this adventure."

They hugged until Ivy's yell broke them up. "Lyra, look at your hair!" She was pointing at them from farther down the path. "You've bonded!"

Misty picked up a strand of Lyra's long hair with her muzzle. It had turned the same purple and spring green as her mane. "We really have!"

she said, nuzzling Lyra. "It's official. We're best friends forever!"

"And partners in adventure?" Lyra said hopefully.

"And partners in adventure!" Misty echoed happily.

Everyone hurried up the path to congratulate them. Beside them the waterfall fell in a thundering sheet of sparkling water.

"I guess we're going to have to walk home," said Sienna, looking at the wrecked raft floating away down the river.

"And we didn't find the map," said Ivy sadly.

"The glittering wall must be farther down the river," said Evie.

"Unless . . ." Lyra pointed to the waterfall. "A glittering wall! Don't you see? That's what the waterfall is. Could the map be hidden behind it?"

They all stared at the sheet of water cascading down. It did look like a wall. From where they were standing, they could just make out a space behind it and a narrow rocky ledge.

"Do you think the map piece might be somewhere along that ledge?" Evie asked.

"Yes!" cried Sienna, who had gone closer to the waterfall. She motioned toward a boulder at the edge of the path. "There's a carving of Daybreak here and an arrow pointing toward it."

"I bet it's there," said Lyra.

"I'm going to look." She glanced at Misty, wondering if she would try to stop her, but Misty just nodded.

"I'll protect you if you slip," she said.

Lyra felt a warm glow. She trusted Misty completely.

"I'll come too," said Sienna quickly.

"And me!" said both Ivy and Evie.

Misty shook her head. "No, please don't. I'm too tired to save all of you if anything goes wrong."

"I'll be fine. Let me go alone," said Lyra.

Her friends didn't look happy but gave in.

"Okay, but be careful," Sienna said.

"I will," promised Lyra.

Dropping to her hands and knees, she crawled out onto the ledge. The water thundered down in front of her, the spray soaking her all over again. The ledge was wet and slippery, and Lyra's heart raced as she inched along it. It grew even nar-

rower, but she could see a small cave just ahead. She was sure that was where she needed to go. She gritted her teeth and kept going until she reached the entrance and crawled inside.

Getting to her feet, she stood up. Her legs were shaky, and she was breathing hard. With her back to the water, she shone her flashlight around the cave. There was nothing there except for a pile of boulders at the back.

Lyra went over to examine them. A perfectly round boulder was balanced on the top. It had an egg-shaped hole in the middle. Lyra poked a finger inside and heard the crackle of paper. Yes! Her heart did somersaults as she teased the paper out and carefully unrolled it.

It was the second piece of the map! There was a picture of Daybreak, the crying unicorn, in the top right corner. The rest of the school was in the top left, and more of the maze was in the bottom

left corner. In the bottom right corner were drawings of some strange stones. Turning it over, Lyra saw a new riddle to solve.

She rolled the paper up and tucked it inside her jacket. They could figure it out later. Right now she needed to get back to safety.

Lyra crawled carefully along the ledge. "I found it!" she gasped as she reached the path and her friends. "We have the second piece!"

Misty's eyes shone as everyone whooped and cheered.

Evie looked thoughtful. "The treasure must be really valuable for someone to go to so much trouble to hide the map."

"We can't tell anyone else," said Sienna.

Lyra nodded. "Let's all promise to keep it our secret."

"I promise!" everyone chorused.

"Should we take the new piece of map back

to our dorm and look at it there?" suggested Lyra. "We don't want it to get wet or fall into the river."

"Agreed," said Sienna as she vaulted onto Sparkle. "Come on!"

Lyra was too excited to mind that Sienna and Sparkle took the lead. She couldn't wait to examine the map and figure out the next clue.

They returned to the stable yard just as Sam, Nawaz, Archie, and Reuben arrived to get their unicorns ready for the treasure hunt.

Sam was carrying two huge bags of warm pastries. He stared at the girls. "You're up even earlier than us. Did you skip breakfast to get a head start on the treasure hunt?"

Lyra shook her head. "We just wanted to take our unicorns for a walk. The gardens are so beautiful." She met Sam's eye, hoping that he'd believe her.

Reuben grinned. "I didn't realize you girls were into nature. I love going for early-morning walks on my grandparents' farm."

Sam held out one of the bags of pastries. "We got these from the kitchen for our breakfast, but there's plenty to go around," he said. "Go on, you can have some. We're dorm neighbors, after all. You must be hungry after your early start."

The other boys nodded.

"Wow! Thanks," the girls said in unison.

Lyra's eyes met Sam's, and he smiled. She smiled back. She didn't understand him at all. Just when she was convinced he was their enemy and wanted the map for his aunt, he did something really nice like this.

"See you on the treasure hunt," said Reuben as the girls each took a warm pastry.

Sam gave Lyra a look that was hard to read.

"Be prepared to lose! We're going to beat you to the treasure today!" he said.

"You bet we are!" said Archie. "First place is as good as ours!"

The boys high-fived each other, then disappeared inside the stables to find their unicorns.

"We need to get ready," said Sienna, watching the boys go.

"I'm tired," Sparkle said.

"Me too," said Misty.

"We could always have breakfast and a rest first," said Ivy.

"But then the boys will have a head start," argued Sienna. "And all the others too." She pointed to more students who were hurrying to the stables.

"So what if they do?" said Lyra. "As soon as we find the rest of the map, we'll have a *real* treasure

hunt to go on. That has to be better than a pretend treasure hunt!" She nudged Sienna. "Come on, you know I'm right."

A grin spread across Sienna's face. "Okay, I guess you are. Breakfast it is!"

They got buckets of sky berries for the unicorns. Then they went to a quiet spot at the back of the stables and sat down to have their mini feast. The pastries were fresh, with gooey fillings and drizzles of white icing.

"Yum!" Lyra smiled as she finished her pastry. Licking crumbs from her fingers, she went over to hug Misty, who was grazing nearby. "Oh, Misty, last night I was so unhappy, and now I'm happier than I've ever been."

Misty nuzzled her. "Me too. Look at my magic!" She stamped her hoof, showering Lyra in purple sparkles. A stream of glittering, multicolored bubbles rose up around them. "Isn't it cool?"

"It's amazing!" Lyra said, feeling like she might burst with happiness. Now that she was sure that she and Misty would graduate at the end of the year, she could relax and enjoy all the adventures that Unicorn Academy had to offer. She couldn't wait to find the next piece of the map. "I love being here with you," she said.

Misty stamped her hoof, and the bubbles burst into a rainbow of fireworks. "It really is magic!" she whinnied.

All sorts of accidents are happening around Unicorn Academy. Can Evie and Sunshine work together to find out why?

Read on for a peek at the next book in the Unicorn Academy Treasure Hunt series!

Unicorn Academy Treasure Hunt: Evie and Sunshine excerpt
text copyright © 2021 by Julie Sykes and Linda Chapman.
Cover art and excerpt illustrations
copyright © 2021 by Lucy Truman.
Published by Random House Children's Books,
a division of Penguin Random House LLC, New York.
Originally published in paperback in the United Kingdom
by Nosy Crow Ltd, London, in 2021.

"That was yummy," Evie said as she licked crumbs of chocolate cake from her fingers. The girls from Ruby dorm were having a picnic while their unicorns grazed on the lush grass. It was late spring, and the apple trees were covered with white blossoms. The bright sunlight, shining through the branches, warmed Evie's face.

"Okay," said Lyra, packing away the picnic things and double-checking that no one else was around. "Now for the important business that we came here to discuss."

"To solve the riddle on the treasure map!" said Sienna. She poked Ivy, who was lying on her back with her eyes shut. "Ivy, wake up!"

Ivy wiggled away. "I am awake. Do you have the map, Lyra?" She rolled onto her stomach.

Lyra carefully pulled two yellowed squares

of paper from her pocket. They crackled as she unfolded them and smoothed them out, placing them side by side on the picnic blanket. Each one was part of a map that had been cut into four pieces. These two each had a small picture of a crying unicorn in their outside corners. Together they made up the top half of the map. They formed a picture of Unicorn Academy and, farther down, part of a maze with half a big X in the center. The girls didn't know what the treasure at the X was, but they were determined to find out!

They had discovered the first piece hidden in a secret room above their dorm. A riddle on the back had led them to the second piece, which they had found behind an underground waterfall on the school grounds. They hoped that the riddle written on it would lead them to the third piece.

"This riddle is really annoying!" said Lyra. "What does it even mean?"

Evie pushed her wavy brown hair behind her ears. She had already memorized the riddle and recited it for the others:

"In a new folly that phantoms keep safe,

There's a space you can enter and leave with no trace.

A cold place to rest hides the circular key,

Press once and enter the d-da-dark cavity."

As Evie stumbled over the last few words, she blushed. Sometimes her mouth just couldn't seem to keep up with her brain and her words came out muddled. Luckily her friends never mentioned it, but she hated when it happened. She also tripped all the time when she was moving fast or playing sports. Evie didn't really mind not being great at sports—she liked reading more and wanted to be a scientist when she was older.

"I don't understand the first line," said Sienna.

"Phantoms are ghosts. But how can ghosts keep anywhere safe?"

"And what's 'a new folly'?" asked Ivy.

"*Folly* means foolish," said Evie.

"A new foolish that ghosts keep safe?" said Lyra. "That doesn't make any sense." She rubbed her forehead in frustration.

The word *folly* was bothering Evie too. She'd heard it before and thought it had another meaning, but she couldn't remember what.

"A cavity's a hole," said Sienna. "Could the dark cavity be the secret room where we found the first part of the map? You have to press a hidden circular button to open it up." Her eyes lit up. "Maybe that's it!"

MeRMiCORns

Swim into a new series!

MeRMiCORns
1

Sparkle Magic

Sudipta Bardhan-Quallen

Mermicorns are part unicorn, part mermaid, and totally magical!

PuRRmaids

Meet your newest feline friends!

PuRRmaids

1

The Scaredy Cat

Sudipta Bardhan-Quallen

Cover art copyright © 2019 by Andrew Farley. Purrmaids® is a registered trademark of KIKIDOODLE LLC and is used under license from KIKIDOODLE LLC.

1277a

rhcbooks.com RHCB

New friends. New adventures.
Find a new series... just for you!

ISADORA MOON
For ballerina and fairy and vampire lovers

MAGIC ON THE MAP
For adventurers

UNICORN ACADEMY
For unicorn lovers

PUPPY PIRATES
For dog lovers

PuRRmaids
For mermaid and cat lovers

BALLPARK Mysteries
For sports fans

Isadora Moon: cover art © Harriet Muncaster. Magic on the Map: cover art © Stevie Lewis. Unicorn Academy: cover art © Lucy Truman. Puppy Pirates: cover art © Luz Tapia. Purrmaids: cover art © Andrew Farley. Purrmaids® is a registered trademark of KIKIDOODLE LLC and is used under license from KIKIDOODLE LLC. Ballpark Mysteries: cover art © Mark Meyers.

rhcbooks.com

⌒ Collect all the books in the ⌒
Horse Diaries series!